S0-ALG-597

*To Caylah
happy reading!
best,
Martha Tolles*

GROWING UP STORIES

BY MARTHA TOLLES

WText copyright © 2013 Martha Tolles

All rights reserved.

ISBN-13: 9781492321644
ISBN: 1492321648
Library of Congress Control Number: 2013916150
CreateSpace Independent Publishing Platform
North Charleston, South Carolina

To dear, smart Peter and my wonderful family

books by Martha Tolles

Secret Sister
Marrying Off Mom
Darci In Cabin 13
Darci and The Dance Contest
Who's Reading Darci's Diary
Katie's Babysitting Job
Katie For President
Katie and Those Boys
Too Many Boys
Pockets Full of Gold
What Happens to the Dog
When Rudy Crowed
Ben's Big Year

TABLE OF CONTENTS

PART 1

BEAR WATCH

By Martha Tolles

Gita and her father were working in their field in Northern India. They were picking corn as fast as they could to bring in the much needed crop.

"Hurry, Gita. Gather the corn faster if you can," Gita's father urged.

"Yes, father. I'll try." Gita stretched high to reach the ears of corn on the tall stalks. She was already hot and perspiring in the warm, late afternoon. But she knew she must keep going, that nightfall meant danger. The big, black Himalayan bears would come out of the forest and try to eat the whole crop if they got a chance. Then she and Mother and Father and new baby brother, Dalip, would go hungry.

But father was slowing down, she noticed with worry. She must work faster then. Always, she tried to show her parents they shouldn't be disappointed in her. Her fingers were strong and quick. Couldn't she do as well as any boy?

"Will you guard the field again tonight, father?" Gita glanced toward their "bear-watch" in the corn field. It was a small platform hut built high up on stilts off the ground. Like other farmers here in Kishtwar in northern India, her father spent many summer nights in the hut. There he would scare the bears away to save the crop.

1

But Father didn't answer. Suddenly he clutched his side and groaned. "Oh, Gita." He dropped the basket of corn and hunched over.

"Father, is it the sickness again?" Gita's fear felt like a rock in her stomach.

"Yes." Father moaned and moved slowly toward the house. Gita hurried after him. "Bring the basket of corn, Gita,"

Already, the question was forming in Gita's mind. Would Father be well by tonight? As they approached the house, Gita saw her mother up on the sod roof, shaking grain back and forth on a big tray. "Mother," Gita called. "Father is ill."

Her mother set down the tray, then picked up baby Dalip. Holding him with one arm, she climbed down the ladder. "What's the matter?" Worry lines creased her forehead. Her gold nose ring gleamed in the sun.

"The sickness," Father said in a choked voice. He stumbled into the house and over to his bed. He groaned. "Tonight the bears...I must be out there." He broke off. Drops of sweat covered his forehead. Gita knew what her father meant. Who would guard the field against the bear? The bear that weighed as much as four men and could swat a man down like an insect.

"Gita," Mother said in a low voice. "I must prepare some medicine." She laid Dalip down in his little bed, then stirred some herbs in a pot over the fire. Then she gave the healing brew to Father. He managed to swallow it, but he moaned again, his whole body bent with pain.

"Won't Father be all right?" Gita had to know.

"Yes, Gita. This is good medicine. But it will take rest and time.

Time. That was the trouble. There was no time. Gita hurried to the doorway. On the hillsides she could already see the farmers' torches flickering like giant bugs among the fields and trees. The greedy bears had to be kept away. Gita shivered with fear. She turned back inside. "Mother," she asked, "who will go out to the bear watch tonight? Someone needs to guard our crop." They both knew that was true. Last year the bears had eaten some of their corn, and there was barely enough food to last through the winter.

"I can't leave baby Dalip all night," Mother said. She looked very tired as she began to prepare their supper. Gita doubted her mother could stay awake all night either. She was still so worn out from having the new baby. And now that meant another mouth to feed.

"Maybe I could go out there," Gita blurted it out, hardly realizing what she was saying.

"What? Gita, you?" Mother's face darkened with fear. "Gita, you are a girl with a little voice. Only nine years old. If a bear came you would have to make a lot of noise. That's foolish talk."

Her mother turned to chopping vegetables, then dropped them in a pot over the fire. Gita wanted to argue, but knew her mother wouldn't like it. She longed to say that she, Gita, could yell good and loud as any boy and that she'd be safe up high in the bear hut.

Gita was so worried she couldn't eat and later in bed, couldn't sleep. As she lay there she could hear her mother's deep breathing and occasional moans from her father. From outside came the warning shouts of the farmers in the nearby fields. But there was no one to guard Gita's family's fields. She, Gita, must do it. She rose and crept quietly as a mouse so no one would hear her. Seeing her pot of leftover supper, she picked it up and took it with her.

"I'll be all right." Gita told herself as she stepped out the door. What would it be like out there all through the night? She tried not to think.

In the cornfield, she walked carefully and listened. But there was no sound, no bear rustling among the cornstalks. Even so, her legsshook with each step.

What if the bear were behind that stalk or that one?

At last she reached the little hut up on stilts, the "bear watch". Quickly she pulled down the ladder and, grasping the pot, she managed to climb up into the hut.

She set down her supper and kneeled on the floor, feeling safer up here high above the ground. She listened for another moment, but all was quiet. So she opened the pot and ate the delicious food.

Then she sat, looking down at the cornfield and listening intently. It was eerily silent and was getting late. The moon had risen, and in its white brightness Gita could see the cornstalks standing in straight rows, many of them, still loaded with the ripe ears of corn. The owl's hoot penetrated the darkness and the steady drone of crickets hummed loudly in her ears.

But what was that? A rustling at the edge of the cornfield! A huge black shape. She could see the hulk moving in the moonlight.

"Oh, please," she prayed. "The bear must be stopped. What shall I do?" There were many thick shadows, but still, Gita could hear that loud scrunching of leaves and stalks. Fear swept through her. But she couldn't just sit there. The bear was out there crunching his way heavily, hungrily through their field.

Gita felt the tears well up in her eyes. She and her whole family would have empty stomachs again this winter. And what if the bear came over here, right here to this "bear watch"?

She shivered, feeling desperate. What could she do? She yelled then, making her voice as big and fierce as she could. "Bear, Bear, go away, Bear! You can't have our corn!"

Still, she heard him scrunching through the corn stalks. Suddenly she remembered what the farmers did sometimes. She reached behind her for her supper pan and the lid and banged them together loudly and shouted again. She did this over and over until she was hot and tired, and her arms and throat ached. Then she stopped to listen, peering out into the darkness. She could hear the bear smashing and crashing his way through the field. But now he was lumbering away up toward the mountain. After a few minutes she could no longer see or hear him.

"He's gone," she shouted joyfully and fell back, hugging her knees. She, Gita, had scared the bear away. She listened again and heard nothing. The moon spilled its silver over the vast Himalayan mountain and her house looked dark and quiet. She sat hunched in her jacket for a long time and finally slept.

When the first light came she awoke, and the cornfield stood thick and untouched. Gita arose, stiff and chilled, but the rosy glow of dawn lightened the air. She threw down the ladder, climbed out, and hurried toward the house. Her father was standing in the doorway smiling at her. Behind him stood her mother, holding baby Dalip in her arms. Gita walked proudly toward them.

There would be bread and yoghurt and honey for breakfast.

THE END

THE ENEMY AND ME

By Martha Tolles

Our Yankee feet are marching through Georgia, stomping and thumping along. We're here with General Sherman's army and we're determined to beat the southern Rebels. But my stomach rumbles and aches for a good meal.

"Can we go look for food?" I ask Sergeant Wilton.

"Not here, Jeremy. There might be Rebs around."

I keep looking around nervously as we march on. I certainly don't want to meet any Rebs. I think about my Ma's good stews and berry pies instead.

When she heard I was going to sign up she threw her apron over her face and cried, "Jeremy. You're only fourteen."

"But President Lincoln needs him," Pa argued. "Lincoln is trying to save the Union. And slavery is a curse on this land."

In town I joined up. I look older than my years.

Now I am here and the weather is cold and rainy and the roads are full of water. We come to a place where we have to wade through a whole lot of muck and mud and slush, but we push on. I'm wet and shivering and I itch all over from the bugs in my uniform. And my empty stomach aches for food.

5

"I'm about starved," I tell my friend, Billy.

"Me too," he agrees.

Night comes on and it's dark as black cats in a cellar. At last we're clear of the trees and up on high ground.

We stop to make camp. We build a fire with pine logs and warm ourselves. "Shake your clothes out over the flames," Billy says to me. The vermin and the bugs fall out like hail and sizzle and burn in the flames.

We have only hard tack with coffee and sugar for supper. But afterwards a soldier named Eddy plays his harmonica and we all listen to the Fireman's Polka, Tenting on the old Campground, Beautiful Dreamer and Aura Lee and then Billy and I fall asleep in our tent.

The next morning breakfast is the same, hard tack and black coffee and we slog along again, always keeping a sharp eye out for Rebs. When we come to some railroad tracks, Sergeant Wilton calls out, "Tear'em up. Burn'em. No supplies or men are coming through on these tracks." We heap up the wooden ties and set fire to them and twist and bend the steel. We choke in the smoky air.

But those Rebs try to stop us too. At the river's edge we discover they've buried explosives under the soil. But we dig them up before they can explode.

And the Rebs float burning logs down the river. "Build a pontoon bridge," the Sergeant orders. From our supply wagons we unload pontoon boats and soon we have a bridge and we walk across very carefully.

The Sergeant lets us make camp early that night. At last he says, "We'll forage for food."

"Let me go," I urge.

"And me," Billy adds.

"All right," Sergeant Wilton agrees. "Stay close. Watch out for Rebs."

We set out with a large group of other soldiers but then Billy and I decide to go off by ourselves so we can be quieter.

We walk through the shadowy, dark woods and we keep looking around. I feel sweaty and nervous.

Suddenly we come to a clearing and there before us is the shell of a large house, charred to the ground, no roof left, blackened walls. One defiant stone chimney still stands. Our soldiers have been here ahead of us.

Billy shakes his head. "I hope the owners aren't around.." We circle around to the back, half hiding behind bushes. We see a few small sheds and cabins.

I spot a hen house, half hidden by some bushes. "I'll go there," I whisper.

"Holler if you need help," Billy says. "I'll hunt around nearby."

I slip through the trees, quiet as a fox. I imagine a bush moves. Is there a Reb behind it? I freeze, cold with fear. But there's only silence.

I breathe and move on. I sneak across the yard to the hen house. I pull open the wooden door. Two hens cackle noisily. What if some Reb hears? But I see fresh eggs in the nests. I quickly put the eggs in my cap. Then I grab the two hens by their legs. Squawk, squawk! They are so loud. I struggle to hold them with one hand and my cap with the other.

The door creaks sharply. I whirl around, my heart jumping. There in the doorway is a girl, bone thin. She clutches a shawl around sharp shoulders and her eyes are filled with hate and fear.

"We need those hens." Her voice is urgent. "They're near about all we have left."

"Our soldiers are hungry," I exclaim. I start past her, carrying the hens and the eggs. I'm so close I see how tattered her old dress is.

"My mother has to have them," she says.

"Our soldiers need food," I retort. I can't go back empty handed.

Then she grabs at the two squawking hens. "Let go."

I try to pull the hens away.

But she pulls harder. The hens cluck wildly.

Suddenly through the dusky air comes a squalling cry. "Is that a baby?" I exclaim.

She nods. "My brother. He's just born."

I stand there, stunned for a moment. A new baby? A mother, weak and needing food for herself and the baby...and this poor half starved girl...these folks are the enemy? They're suffering just like us. Such a strong feeling sweeps over me. Pity? Sympathy? I don't know what.

"Here, you need these hens worsen we do, I reckon." I let go.

"Oh, thank you." She sounds grateful.I step outside. At least I have the eggs to take to camp. I go back through the woods. Darkness is creeping over the sky. I feel a pain in my heart and a stinging in my eyes. How I wish there would be an end to this war soon.

The war did end a few months later and many feel that General Sherman's march through the south helped bring that about.

THE END

THE DOLL AND THE INDIAN
By Martha Tolles

The slow-moving wagon train swung into a circle with wonderful preci-
sion and stopped near the broad Platte River. Here was a fine campsite
with plenty of grass and firewood. Penelope gathered up her beloved
rag doll and scrambled down from her wagon. My, how good it felt to
run and skip after the day's long drive! And how many more days there
would be before they reached Oregon!

"Quick, Penelope, get over yonder," her father shouted.

Penelope moved hastily out of the way of the oxen that were being
unyoked and driven out for grass and water so they would be ready and
strong for the next day's long pull over the Oregon Trail. Sometimes,
it seemed to Penelope, the oxen were the most important part of the
whole wagon train. When one had vanished during the night, the folks
wore long faces and blamed the Indians. Now that they were deep in
Sioux territory, two guards were posted every night to watch over the
oxen. For how could they travel without these broad beasts?

Forgetting about the oxen, Penelope skipped again and bumped
right into her good friend Molly.

"Where're you going, Penelope?" Molly laughed.

"Just taking my doll for a walk," Penelope answered airily. No one else had such a nice doll. She held it up for Molly to admire again. Aunt Nell had spent days working on the doll, stuffing it with cornhusks, painting the face, and then making clothes.

"She's mighty pretty," Molly said wistfully, as she admired the doll's blue print dress, white sun bonnet, and yellow yarn hair. I wish I had one just like her."

All around, a hubbub of activity commenced as the travelers began to build their fires and prepare supper. Soon the air was filled with the smell of biscuits and roasting buffalo meat. The men had been lucky to shoot buffalo that day. They would have a good meal tonight. Tomorrow the travelers would spend the day drying the meat in strips and packing it in their wagons. Later, food would be scarce.

Thinking of all this, Penelope remembered that she soon would have to help with the supper.

"Come on, Molly," she said, "it's still daylight. Let's walk outside the circle for a few minutes."

The two girls slipped beyond the circle and picked the pretty yellow wild flowers growing in the tall grass. They ran here and there until Penelope almost stumbled into a tiny stream. They bent down to drink the sparkling water. How delicious it was after the day's hot drive! They drank and drank, and splashed their hands and faces. But when they started to get up, they gasped in dismay.

There, on a crest of ground above them, stood an Indian. Beside him was a little Indian girl on a pony.

"Oh, oh!" gasped Molly.

"My goodness!" Penelope exclaimed and quickly snatched up her doll which she had laid on the ground while she drank.

For a short time they all stood staring at each other in surprise. Then the Indian advanced slowly, leading the pony behind him. Penelope glanced nervously over her shoulder. She was not greatly frightened since the wagon train was near. The Indian came closer and spoke a few words.

"I'm sorry, but we can't understand you," Penelope answered. Then, not knowing what else to do, she curtsied as she had been properly taught.

The Indian and the little girl spoke a few words to each other, while Molly and Penelope looked at the Indian girl curiously. How easily she sat on the pony! How different she looked in her deerskin dress with her long, black braids!

The Indian girl's round dark eyes were fixed on them, too. After a moment Penelope realized that the girl was staring intently at her doll. She proudly held it up for the Indian girl to admire. Then the Indian spoke again at length.

"I don't know what he's saying," Molly whispered nervously. "Think we'd better run to the wagons?" But the Indian went on speaking.

He pointed to the yellow flowers the girls had left by the stream. He waved his arms toward the wagon train. It seemed suddenly to Penelope as though he were saying, "Enjoy my country, the beautiful flowers, the sweet water, the comfortable campsite, the good buffalo meat." For it was his country, wasn't it? He gestured towards the bluffs in the direction of tomorrow's journey as though he wished them safe passage to Oregon.

Penelope had heard her elders talk, and she knew the Indians often resented the pioneers' increasing flow of wagons across their lands. The Indian finished speaking and stood silent. The girl continued to stare at the doll.

Penelope surprised even herself by the unexpected thing she did next. Impulsively, she stepped forward and handed her doll up to the Indian girl.

"It's for you," she said to the Indian girl, who smiled at her. Then Penelope turned and ran back to the wagons with Molly at her heels.

That night was very peaceful. In the morning Penelope discovered something strange. On the edge of the wagon in which she and her mother and father had slept all night, there lay a little Indian doll in a deerskin dress. It looked almost like the Indian girl.

THE END

WHO WILL BE EMPEROR
(A CHINESE LEGEND)
By Martha Tolles

Long ago in ancient China Wan Chun was working one day in his small garden by the river. Suddenly he was startled by the sound of horse's hooves thumping down the road. There was a horseman on a black steed approaching and as he drew near Wan Chun could see he carried a banner from the emperor.

"I have an announcement from the emperor," the messenger called, skidding to a stop in a swirl of dust. "Listen carefully. The emperor wants you to plant these seeds." He tossed a packet out to Wan Chun's outstretched hands. "Whichever boy in the whole of China grows the brightest flowers will be the next emperor." Then, he was off, galloping at top speed to spread the word.

Wan Chun was thrilled. He hurried home to tell his family the exciting news. His Baba (Father) and his Mama were so happy too. "Yes, yes, you must plant the seeds and grow the best flowers possible," they agreed.

So Wan Chun planted the seeds in long rows. Then he waited and watched and shooed the birds away. But the garden remained bare and one day he suddenly heard a shout. It was How-Yo, the big, boastful neighbor's boy who lived over the hill.

"What's wrong with you garden?" He pointed scornfully at the bare ground. "Is nothing growing in it? Didn't you plant the emperor's seeds?"

"Yes, of course I did." Wan Chun stood tall and spoke up to How-Yo who towered over him.

"Did you? How is your garden?"

"Mine has long rows of green shoots, green as jade and very healthy. I will have beautiful flowers and I will be emperor some day. You'll see." How-Yo smirked with pride and sauntered off over the hill.

Wan Chun watched him go and felt sick at heart to hear this news. What could he do? He must work harder, from rosy dawn to purple dusk.

Each day Wan Chun pulled out greedy weeds from his garden. He sprinkled the dry soil with nourishing river water and scared off the seed-hungry birds when they swooped down from the sky.

But it was difficult to keep them away so he went to his mother. "Mama, do you think I might use some of my old clothes to make a scarecrow?"

"Yes, my son." His mother looked up from the baby she held in her arms. "But remember, later we will need your clothes for this little one."

He hurried to hang his old blue jacket and red pants on a post at the edge of the garden to frighten away the birds. And he dreamed that soon there would be rows of tender shoots, then beautiful blossoms and he would be chosen to be emperor. Then there would be enough rice for the little one, a shining jade for his mother, a chance to rest for his father.

But one golden day after another slipped by and Wan Chun watched and waited. The dirt square remained as barren as ever. And how was How-Yo's garden doing, Wan Chun wondered. Were his green shoots growing tall, perhaps turning into bright buds by now?

Finally, in despair Wan Chun dug up a few of the seeds he'd planted. He was stunned to find they were just the same as when he had put them in the ground, hard, dry, brown without even the tiniest green sprouts on them.

His eyes burned with disappointment. Sadly, that evening he showed them to his family as they ate from their rice bowls. "What shall I do?" he asked. But his parents didn't know.

Still, he tended his barren garden, trying not to think of How-Yo's garden which must be crowded with blossoms by now.

In late summer the emperor sent out his messenger on his black steed to summon all the young gardeners to his palace.

'I wish I didn't have to go," Wan Chun told his father. His father didn't answer, just waited for him to continue. So he straightened his shoulders. "But I know I must."

"That's right, that's the honorable way." His father looked approving now.

So, empty-handed, Wan Chun set off but his steps were slow and sad, and even slower and sadder after he met How-Yo. "See my flowers," boasted How-Yo, carrying an armful of the biggest, reddest peonies Wan Chun had ever seen. "Where are yours?"

Wan Chun didn't answer. He just walked ever more slowly, especially after he met crowds of other young people hurrying toward the palace. They were all carrying armloads of colorful blossoms, pinks and reds and whites and lavenders.

At the palace the emperor sat in his silks and satins and looked solemnly out at the flower-decked crowd. "I am old and weary. I have no sons and I must find a successor," he spoke slowly. "What have you to report?"

One by one each gardener stepped forward, bowed low and said, "Your Honor, I have a most beautiful garden with many bright peonies and other flowers, thanks to your fine seeds." Each garden, it seemed, was better than the last.

Finally it was Wan Chun's turn. How hurtful it was going to be to admit he was such a failure.

Wan Chun moved forward and stooped very low before the emperor "Your Highness." He spoke in almost a whisper. "My garden did not grow." He trembled with shame.

"What? What's that you say?" The emperor leaned forward. "Speak up."

Wan Chun took a deep breath. "The seeds did not sprout, Kind Highness. I worked hard and watered and watched and drove away the hungry birds but nothing grew. I am sorry." He hung his head even lower.

To his complete astonishment, the emperor rose shakily from his throne and flung open his arms. "Hear ye, hear ye. Now I present to you my successor, the next emperor." Wan Chun stared in amazement as the emperor beckoned to his aides to come forward and lift Wan Chun up onto the throne. And then they placed ajeweled crown on his head and the trumpeters blasted their music to the rooftop of the palace.

"But, Kind Emperor." Wan Chun tried to keep bowing and yet hold onto the crown on his head. "Why have you chosen me when my garden didn't produce a single flower?"

"Because, you see," the emperor turned to the crowd. "These seeds which I sent to all of you, I had first cooked in boiling oil so they would not grow. I was hoping to find an honorable lad, one who would speak the truth, to succeed me." He paused for a moment as a sigh swept over the crowd and many faces turned red with embarrassment.

"But I found only one, this young lad here, who admitted he had no flowers. The truth is the brightest flower of all. Never forget that."

The trumpets blared again and Wan Chun sat straight and proudly on the throne for now he knew he had at least one flower after all, the flower of truth.

THE END

PART 11

ABOUT BOYS

RIVER CAMP

By Martha Tolles

We pull our motorboat up on a sandy beach on the Colorado River. It's a good spot for our camp. Right away I'm looking at the rocky cliffs and hills around us. "I hope I can get a picture of a bighorn sheep," I tell my dad and my older brother, Mark.

"Those sheep have special hooves so they can climb up steep, rocky places," Mark says.

"Yes, they stay far out of sight," Dad added.

I'll try anyway. My mom gave me a camera for my twelfth birthday and I hang it around my neck.

After we finish putting up the tent my dad says, "Time to catch some fish for supper. Let's fish right off shore here." I know that means sitting still for a while.

So I say, "Can Blackie and I go for a hike? I could take a few pictures?" My dog, Blackie, barks. That probably means yes, let's go.

Dad frowns. "Stay along the beach where we can see you. And take care of yourselves."

"I promise. Come on, Blackie." We start off. The long stretch of sandy shore stretches out before us, the shining river on one side, the rocky cliffs and bare hills on the other. I snap a couple of pictures.

Then I take one of the beach. It's dotted with big rocks here and there and clumps of Brittle bushes.

Suddenly Blackie barks and runs toward something. It looks like a snake, a rattler. "Blackie, stop," I shout.

But he's already there, nose to the ground. Before I can reach him a sudden breeze makes the snake fly up in the air a bit. It's only the snake's skin. He's shed it a while ago. I lean over and touch it. It's dry and there is the bony rattler in its tail. I want to take it with me but Dad always says leave the desert as you found it. Instead, I snap a picture of it. I'll show it to my science class.

Just then Blackie barks again. He's leaping up at a big rock. I run over there. A little mouse skitters up the side of the rock. "Oh, Blackie leave the mouse alone. Come on." I quick snap a picture of the mouse, and I pull Blackie by the collar away from there. We keep on walking and I stare at the cliffs, hoping to see a big horn. I know they're scarce and hard to find but great looking with really huge horns. Blackie's running ahead again, sniffing something. I run to catch up. This time it's some droppings. They're big, so probably a desert mule. I decide not to take a picture of that. I'd like to see the mule though.

Suddenly Blackie darts off. Now he's chasing a long-eared brown rabbit. "Come back, Blackie," I shout but he keeps on running. I yell some more. "Blackie, don't hurt that rabbit." But he runs farther away and on into the bushes. Now I can't even see him. But I hear the hoarse cry of a bird over head. There is a black hawk circling. Is he after the rabbit? Oh, no, maybe he's after Blackie. Blackie's still a puppy, not that big yet. I know hawks can catch baby chicks.

"Blackie," I bawl after him but he doesn't come. "I have to get Blackie," I call back to Mark and Dad but I don't know if they heard me. I start chasing after Blackie and yell some more and I run where I see sand flying up in the air. There's a breeze now and the sand keeps whirling around.

I run and run and finally I see Blackie. He's coming toward me now. The rabbit must have gone into its burrow in the ground. "Bad dog," I scold Blackie. "We've gotta get back." But as I turn around oh, whoa.....a huge blast of sand whams into me. I have to close my eyes and cover my face. I try to move forward but now there's sand blowing like crazy everywhere. I can't see, can't look, and the sand stings and hurts. I don't know which way to go. Blackie crouches next to me and whimpers. I lean down and grab him by the collar. We have to get out of this. Through my squeezed up eyes I see some big rocks. I drag Blackie that way and we crouch down between the rocks. I close my eyes because some sand gets in behind the rocks too.

We wait and wait. Mark and Dad will come looking for us soon as they can, I'm sure. "Here we are," I shout into the air. They can't see us so I keep on yelling. "We're here, behind this rock." Maybe they have to wait too for the sand storm to die down. I yell again anyway but nothing happens. Blackie whimpers and snuggles up close to me.

Suddenly I hear the howl of a coyote. What if he comes near us? He might go for Blackie. I sift through the sand and find some stones. I throw them in the direction of that howling coyote. No way is he going to get Blackie. This was bad. How did I ever let us get into such a mess? I promised Dad I'd take good care of Blackie and me.

But just then, "Hallo-o-o-o," I hear. "Where are you?" It's Mark and Dad!

I jump up. "Here, we're right here." They're running toward me with towels over their heads though the sandstorm is dying down now.

They're really happy to see me, Blackie too. "We were worried about you," they say. We get a lot of hugs. And I sure am glad to see them. "I had to go after Blackie," I explain. "He chased a rabbit and I was afraid a hawk would catch him. Then the sand came and I heard a coyote. I'm sorry I went so far away."

I happened to glance toward the rocky hills. "Oh, look," I whispered. "A big horn!" Perched on a ledge, huge horns on its head, it stood. I grabbed my camera, luckily kept safe in its cover, and quickly took a picture, then another and the big horn disappeared.

"Wasn't that lucky?" I exclaimed.

Dad smiled. "You did a good jobhere, taking care of yourselves. So you deserved some luck."

I did? I grinned with pride. That was great Dad thought so. Maybe it was even better than the terrific picture of the big horn.

THE END

NOT A CHERRY TREE

By Martha Tolles

Every day I see the other kids at school playing with their superhero cards. At lunchtime, they kneel in circles on the playground and show their cards to one another. They swap a few and laugh and have fun. I go climb on the bars, but I feel left out. Sometimes Rick and T.J. let me look at their cards. Today they don't let me. "Maybe tomorrow," Rick says. "We're in a hurry." And they rush off to join the others.

Last night, I again asked my mom to buy me some. She said, "Sorry, Mike, honey. I can't right now. Maybe you could put it on your birthday list." My birthday is far away.

Back in class, our second-grade teacher, Miss Grady, says, "Tomorrow we're going to have a little party for a very special person. But it's a surprise."

"Who? Who is it?" we ask. But she just laughs. I like Miss Grady a lot. I like the way she smiles at us. I'm excited about the party, the cake or cookies we might have. It almost makes me stop thinking about those cards. But not quite. The bell rings and we get up to leave.

My seat is in the back row so I'm one of the last out of the room. I notice that Rick has left his desk open and there are his superhero cards. Nobody is around. I don't know what makes me do this, but as I pass by his desk, I reach out and grab the pack. I slip it in my pocket. At last I have some cards.

It's a funny thing though, but all the way to the bus, those cards feel so heavy in my pocket. They weigh me down. I feel as if I'm walking crooked almost. And I realize now I can't take them out and show them around and have fun with them. Everyone would say, "Where'd you get those? Thought you didn't have any."

On the bus, T.J. says, "Wonder who the party is for tomorrow." He looks excited, but it doesn't seem like much fun to me anymore.

When I get home, I hurry to my room and close the door. I dig those cards out of my pocket and spread them on my bed. They really do look great. There's Spider-Man, who catches the bad guys in his web, and Superman with his red cape, and Batman, all in black with an orange belt. They are awesome. How strong and brave they are.

I hear Mom's footsteps. I yank the bedspread over he cards and roll over on top of them.

"My goodness!" Mom stands in the doorway. She looks surprised. "Are you tired already?" She starts to come forwar

I bounce up off my bed. "No, Mom, noWell, come for supper now."

"OK, Mom." As soon as she leaves, I grab those cards and shove them into my bureau drawer.

What if she finds out? I don't even want to think about it. Tonight Mom has made a stew for supper. It's one of my favorites, but I'm not very hungry. I don't feel like talking, either.

"I hope you're not coming down with something," Mom says worriedly.

I know I'm not.

While we eat, Mom asks, "How was your day?"

I stare down at my plate, trying to think of something to say. Then I remember. "We're having a surprise birthday party in our class tomorrow.""How nice." She studies me. "You don't seem very excited about it."

It's hard to be excited when you've got a big cloud hanging over you. But I can't tell her that.

After I'm in bed, Mom reads to me until I finally fall asleep. But it's not peaceful. Suddenly, Superman is racing toward me, his cape flapping behind him. He's glaring at me. "I'll catch you," he shouts.

I try to run, but my feet are like cement blocks. I thrash around, wake up, all tangled in my covers.

In the morning, I load up my backpack with those cards. I have to do something about them, but what?

At school, I see Rick walking around the playground, looking really sad. "Has anybody seen my superhero cards?" he asks. "I saved up my birthday money to buy them."

I hurry off and slump into a swing. I hadn't thought about how bad he'd feel. Everybody else is playing and having fun, climbing on the bars or kicking a ball, except for Rick and me.

T.J. comes over to me. "I hope we have good food at the party today, don't you? I wonder whose party it is."

"I don't know," I say. What I really mean is, I don't know what to do.

The bell rings and I walk slowly toward my classroom. I have to leave my backpack outside the door with the other backpacks. What if someone looks in my pack and sees those cards? I wait till the last minute so everyone else has gone in the room ahead of me. Then I walk in. Right away I see red and blue crepe paper draped across a big picture of George Washington, hanging on the wall. Everyone is looking at it. Now we know whose birthday it is. I hurry over to my desk and sit down. I don't look at Rick as I pass him.

"So now you all know." Miss Grady is smiling. "Washington's birthday is today. I'm going to read to you about him. Then laterwe'll have refreshments." We look at one another. The food sounds OK, but will the reading be good? It turns out it is.

We hear how George Washington and his troops were hungry and cold. But they crossed a river during the night and stole up on the British and drove them away. They were as brave as Superman!

Then Miss Grady reads an old tale about George Washington as a boy. She explains about tales and how they usually aren't true, but they can teach good lessons. In this one, Washington had a hatchet. One day he saw a cherry tree. He chopped it down. We all gasp. We have just one tree on our playground. But when he was asked if he had done it, he said, "I cannot tell a lie." Just then Miss Grady glances up from the book. Is she looking at me?

She closes the book. "So you see, the lesson from this tale is that even the greatest man made some mistakes as a boy."

I've made one too, and I'm shrinking down in my seat, thinking about it.

Just then the door opens, and T.J.'s mother and another lady come in the room, carrying a big box. "Perfect timing!" Miss Grady exclaims. "We're ready for our party."

It's funny how I don't feel hungry. The mothers set out cans of fruit punch. I do feel thirsty. Then they give us each a red plate with blue and white napkins. They pass out big chocolate chip cookies. I eat part of one, but it seems so dry. I keep looking at that picture of George Washington. So he made a mistake. But then he admitted it. And he grew up to be a great man anyway. As my mom would say, "It's hard to be perfect."

Suddenly I straighten up. I have an idea. When the bell rings for recess, I go get my backpack, and then I stay behind in the classroom. Luckily, only Miss Grady is there. I pull out the cards. My hands feel sweaty. Talk fast, I tell myself. "I took Rick's cards yesterday. Now I want to give them back. I'm sorry." I spill it all out. I can't look up at her. She'll probably never smile at me again.

"Why, thank you, Tim." She sounds surprised. "I'll explain to Rick they've been turned in. He'll be so happy. You made a mistake, but you admitted it." I look up, and she is smiling.

I start for the door, picking up another cookie as I go. I give George Washington a thumbs-up as I pass by. Then I race across the playground, eager to start playing. And, hey, at least I didn't chop down a cherry tree.

THE END

BIG SHOT

By Martha Tolles

Robbie bent over his handlebars. He was in a hurry to sign up for a paper route so he would be the most important kid on the block.

Up ahead he saw an older boy, Michael, walking along the sidewalk. And as he passed him, Michael looked up and waved. "Hi, Robbie," he called out. Robbie waved back, pleased to be noticed by an older boy. He had heard that Michael was hoping for a paper route, too.

As he whizzed off down the street, he thought, Michael doesn't even have a bike. How can he do a paper route?

There was a line of boys and girls at Mr. Hansen's house. Mr. Hansen was busy writing down their names. Robbie wondered how many jobs were open for delivering the Evening Standard. Jack and Jennifer had both had routes before. They were sure to get jobs.

When Mr. Hansen got through taking down the names, he said, "I'll let you know in a few days. I need three people for the routes this spring. Thanks for coming." Robbie felt discouraged as he rode home. Jack and Jennifer were sure to get routes. That left just one more. What chance do I have, he thought.

Robbie tried to forget about the paper route the next day. It was another sunny spring day, and played soccer on the playground until it was late.

On the way home he noticed dark clouds piling up in the sky. Soon it began to rain. Thunder grumbled in the distance. Robbie shivered and rode faster.

Then, just as he came to Mr. Hansen's house, he noticed the evening paper lying out near the curb. I ought to put Mr. Hansen's paper on the porch for him, he thought. He jumped off his bike, grabbed the paper, and started for the house. Just then Mr. Hansen came out on his porch.

"Hi, Mr. Hansen." Bobbie hurried toward him. "Here's your paper."

"Why, thanks," Mr. Hansen smiled down at him. "That's nice of you. Say, weren't you here yesterday?"

Robbie nodded, pleased that Mr. Hansen remembered him. "Yes, I was Mr. Hansen looked off into the rain. "I've been thinking about the routes," he said. "I'm giving one to Jack and one to Jennifer. They did a good job before." Robbie held his breath. "I could give the other one to you." Robbie's hopes rose. "Or I could give it to Michael."

"Michael doesn't have a bike," Robbie said before he could stop himself.

"I know," Mr. Hansen nodded. "He's offered to walk the route. That way he could earn money for one."

Robbie glanced through the rain toward his gleaming red racer bike. He had received it as a Christmas gift. Robbie knew what he should do. It would be fun to have a route now, of course. He could see himself flying down the street on his bike, tossing papers on all the lawns, and all the little kids admiring him.

"Let Michael have the route." He looked up at Mr. Hansen. "I'm younger anyway."

Mr. Hansen smiled down at him. "I'll tell you what then. The next route that comes along is yours."

Robbie grinned. "Okay, thanks, Mr. Hansen." It was nice to know that he would have a paper route later, and in the meantime Michael could get his bike.

As Robbie ran through the rain toward his bike, he had the strangest feeling. Somehow, he felt important already.

THE END

Mine

By Martha Tolles

Billy was really excited about the first day of kindergarten. I hope I can make friends," he told his mom.

She smiled. "Of course you will. Remember to share and ask politely for your turn. Your teacher, Miss Tejada, can't help everyone every minute."

But when Billy saw the classroom filled with all kinds of good toys, he couldn't think of anything else. He had to play with them. Fast. Right now. He rushed over to a big fire engine. Another boy was just reaching for it. "My turn," Billy shouted and pushed him aside.

Billy slid the fire engine all around, screeching a noise like a siren. He came to a tall tower of blocks a girl was building. He knocked it down and took the blocks for himself.

"Billy, remember to share," Miss Tejada called from across the room. But Billy didn't listen.

Then he saw a boy holding a big model of a dinosaur. "I need that. Mine," he said and yanked it away from the other boy.

When Miss Tejada took them out to the playground Billy ran to a swing. He swung on it and kicked his feet in the air so no one could come near him and use it.

Miss Tejada was busy helping some boys go down the slide. Then she tossed several balls onto the playground. Billy ran to get one. He pulled it out of a boy's hands.

"Kick it here," others shouted. But Billy just bounced it and kept it for himself.

"Time for a story," Miss Tejada called. Billy still clutched the ball as they ran back inside. They all sat in a circle on the floor. But no one sat next to Billy. "Move closer together," Miss Tejada said. But they only slid a few inches toward Billy.

A girl named Susie leaned toward Billy. "We don't want to sit near you. You grab everything for yourself."

Billy stared at her, stunned. Was that true? He looked around at the circle. No one smiled at him. There were big empty spaces on either side of him. He felt lonesome.

Slowly he rolled the ball toward Susie. "Yours," he said.

THE END

PART III

ABOUT GIRLS

BARN DANCE

By Martha Tolles

I could hardly wait for Jan to visit me. Of all my friends in the City, she was the most fun. I hadn't seen her since we'd moved. I could hear her high, happy laugh already, and I was really eager to tell her about the barn dance we were invited to the next day.

When my dad's car finally came bumping into the driveway, I ran out to meet her. "Jan, it's so great to see you."

"It's great to be here, Sharon." She hugged me. I grabbed her suitcase and her guitar. We clattered all over our farmhouse together, talking every minute. I took her outside to show her the old well under the maple trees. Then we walked over to the fence to watch the cows in the pasture. Jan could move along as fast as I could, in spite of her crippled leg. She managed to do almost everything, ride a bike, play volleyball and even dance.

"Jan, listen." I turned to her. "Would you like to go to a square dance? Our neighbors. the Boones, have invited us."

"Oh, that sounds terrific." Her face broke into a delighted smile.

So that evening. we practiced hooking arms and spinning around. The way Jan moved, no one would know she was crippled at all. Then Jan played the guitar, and we sang and talked. Just before we fell asleep,

Jan said, "It's really nice here, Sharon. I'm so glad I came." I felt the same way.

The next afternoon, we had to get ready for the barn dance. We gave each other manicures and shampooed our hair. We took baths. I tried not to look when Jan removed the brace from her poor, thin leg. Luckily, we both had long skirts.

Dressed at last, we went downstairs. My mom and dad said how nice we looked, and I could see that it was true, for Jan, anyway. She had softness about her face and the curve of her mouth, and there was a shine in her dark eyes.

"Do you think we'll remember the steps?" I said.

"Oh, we will." Jan seemed confident. "That's one good thing about all the hopping and skipping around," she said, laughing, "and with these long skirts nobody will even notice I have a bad leg."

I saw my mother's mouth tighten and my father look away. Jan made them sad. She was happy; couldn't they see that? There was nothing to worry about. "Listen!" I said. I heard the Boone's car coming up the driveway. "Here they come."

"Good-bye," we called, and we hurried out to the car.

The sky was darkening as we set off. The fields were dotted with white Queen Anne's lace and yellow daisies and patches of purple loosestrife. The air was balmy. Mrs. Boone put on the country music station on the radio. "To put you in the mood," she told us.

At last our car turned a long curve. And there was a large red barn outlined against the sky. There were trucks and cars parked all around. As we pulled in, we heard the beat of the music.

In the barn, sets of dancers whirled round and round, doing do-si-dos. A fiddler scraped and swung his bow. The caller, red-faced and smiling, chanted to the crowd. Skirts whirled; feet stomped.

The place was warm, alive, a moving mixture of color and sound.

When there was a break, we joined a group of dancers. They seized our hands, and we swung in a circle, one way, then the other. The music made my feet feel light and free. I was swept up by it. Glancing at Jan's laughing face, I knew she felt the same way. Next, we formed a square, swinging our partners to and fro. Jan skipped into the center to meet an old farmer in overalls, who swung her around neatly. No one would guess that Jan had a problem at all. Her brace never showed.

After a long spell of dancing, there was a pause. We went to the far end of the barn for apple cider and doughnuts. As we sipped ice-cold cider, a tall boy came over to us. "Hi. My name's Bert," he said. Just then, another boy joined him.

"And I'm Dave," the other grinned. He was shorter, with a muscular chest and arms and a tumble of blond hair. I could see he was looking at Jan, and she was looking at him. There seemed to be some instant spark between them. It didn't go away as they danced, either. Even when they changed partners, they seemed to keep looking for each other.

During another break, Dave and Jan slipped outside for air. They didn't ask Bert and me to go along. So Bert and I strolled around the barn together, drinking cider, telling jokes. I introduced him to the Boones. Then it came time for the final round of dances. Jan and Dave came over to join us.

"Swing your partner to and fro, whirl around, and do-si-do," the caller chanted. The fiddler scraped. The rhythm and the thud of feet grew wilder and faster. I wanted it to go on forever. Jan skipped out into the center again to meet the same old farmer in overalls. Her eyes were large and bright. This time, he seized her around the waist. As they spun, he whirled her right off the ground.

Her dark, glossy hair and skirts flew out behind her. And there, for all to see, was the one good leg and the other, thin, leg strapped in the brace. Then he set her down, her skirts falling around her again. She skipped back to Dave. Dave stood waiting. I wondered what the expression on his face meant. I couldn't tell.

"She's quite a little lady," I heard someone say behind me. "Right smart dancer." I felt proud of my friend.

The dance broke up then. We walked outside to find the Boones. Bert was with us, but where was Dave?

"What's your phone number?" Bert was saying. "We could drive over some night." We? But where was the other half? I glanced all around, but there was no Dave. Jan was waiting by the car, alone. We lingered. I could see Jan's eyes searching the faces. I even saw Bert look around once or twice. The Boones kept talking with friends.

The cars and pickup trucks revved up their engines. One after the other, they sped off into the dark night, headlights gleaming. The Boones climbed into their car and started the engine. "Goodbye," we called to Bert. We had to go. The Boones turned on loud music in the car.

I didn't know what to say. Jan did not make a sound, and there wasn't a motion from her corner of the seat. She sat, like a wounded shadow, in the darkness. The night was moonless, with the blackness pressing in all around us.

I yawned loudly. "I'm tired," I said. "How about you, Jan?"

"Oh, yes," Jan said faintly. "Wake me up when we get home, okay?"

That left me riding through the late night, with the Boones talking up front. The music thumped from the radio. The doubts and worries were thick in my mind. Why hadn't Dave shown up? Why? Maybe there was an answer, but I didn't want to think about what it might be.

Then we were home, saying thank you to the Boones, back in the warm, lighted room. My mom and dad were sitting there, their faces eager, as they scanned ours.

"Oh, it was wonderful!" I knew I was talking too loudly. "We had so much fun! We danced and we danced." I was blabbing. But their eyes strayed to Jan's pale face. I know what you're thinking, I wanted to say to them. But don't think it. Maybe we're wrong.

"I'm rather tired," Jan said in a low voice. She started for our bedroom, and I went after her. We undressed, hardly speaking. I quickly pulled a nightgown over my two good legs. What right did I have to be so lucky? I wanted to say something. I thought it would be better to talk. But she said abruptly, "Good night, Sharon." Her voice sounded smothered by the covers, already pulled up around her head. What words could heal a wound? I wanted to go back to yesterday and stay there. I climbed into my bed. But I kept seeing the sadness on my parents' faces. I felt sure I would never sleep that night. I heard my parents moving around downstairs. They were turning off the lights, locking the doors.

Suddenly I heard the phone ring. It was late, so it probably wasn't for us.

But then I heard my mother's voice calling. "Sharon, is Jan still awake? The call's for her."

"Jan?" I whispered.

"I'm awake." I heard Jan getting up from her bed. "Do you suppose it's my parents?"

I heard her go down the hall. I had to know who it was. I threw back my covers and went to the doorway. I heard Jan say hello. I waited. Then I was amazed to hear her laugh. Laugh! And I heard her say, "Oh, Dave, of course, that's all right." I knew then that I shouldn't eavesdrop any longer. I smiled into the darkness and groped my way back to bed. Dave! That's all I wanted to know. I slid under the covers and closed my eyes, still smiling

THE END

BREAKING UP

By Martha Tolles

As I walked toward my locker after school, I caught a glimpse of Mike
through the crowds. Something about the way he was standing and
smiling made me wonder. As I drew closer, I saw he was laughing with
that new girl, Mindy. Her long blonde hair hung almost to her waist,
and the whole scene gave me a scared feeling in my chest. If anything
happened to Mike and me   I had never once let myself think about it.

Mike glanced my way and came toward me. He'd been my boyfriend
all year. "Hi, Mike," I called. So he was talking to Mindy. So what?

"Lisa!" In his letterman's jacket, his shoulders looked broader that
ever. "I want to talk to you."

As we walked toward our favorite bench, many of the other kids
called to us. Everyone knew we went around together. When we reached
the bench, Mike turned to me and took my hands. But he didn't smile.
He stared into the distance and said, "Lisa, I've got to tell you. We
have to break up. You've got to know more guys, and I've got to know
more girls."

I felt a terrible stabbing pain inside. It couldn't be happening!

I don't know what we said after that. He drove me home and walked me to my front door. I never cried. I still couldn't believe it. I guess I thought our love would never end.

I didn't want to tell anybody that I wasn't Mike's girl anymore, not Mom or Dad, not even my best friend, Jill. I didn't want anybody to know I was just plain old Lisa Jordan again.

I said I wasn't hungry at dinnertime and went up to my room. I was going to do my homework, but instead I looked at my pictures of Mike. I should have gone down to help with the dishes, but I wanted to stay in my room. Two years ago, Mom and Dad had given me the money to redecorate my room. I'd had a lot of fun doing it, and now it was my refuge.

I tried to go to sleep that night, but scenes of Mike and me kept coming into my mind, his face and brown eyes smiling down at me the first time we met; the parties we went to; that first kiss, with his arms around me on my doorstep. He was my first real love. He was a top football player and very well-known at school. As his girl, I became well-known, too. I joined more school activities, but I felt that most of all I was known as Mike's girl. Now all that was gone. The next morning, I told Mom I was sick. I couldn't face school. People would know we'd broken up. And how could I bear to see Mike talking and laughing with other girls?

In the afternoon, it began to rain. The whole world seemed to be dripping and weeping. I heard the phone ring, but when Mom came to the door, I pretended to be sleeping. I didn't want to talk to anybody. I knew Mike wouldn't call. Mom brought a tray to my room, and I tried to eat dinner. I could tell she knew something was wrong, but I wanted my privacy. When I was younger, I told her everything, but I was too old for that now.

Somehow I slept and woke and slept again through another night. And all the while the rain poured down outside. When I awoke the next morning, Saturday, and saw the gray daylight, I wished I could go on sleeping and sleeping. I had never felt this far down before.

I heard Mom calling to me from outside my door, and I closed my eyes, ready to feign sleep.

"Lisa." Her voice was urgent. "Jill is on the phone. She sounds very upset."

I opened one eye. Jill? Upset? That didn't sound like her. "Jill says she has to talk to you," Mom went on. "Something bad has happened."

I decided I'd better get up and go out into the hall and answer the phone. "What's the matter, Jill?"

"Oh, Lisa, it's just the worst! You know that rain all night?"

"Uh-huh."

"Well, our roof leaked. It came into my bedroom and down two walls. It ruined my new wallpaper."

Oh, was that all? That was nothing like losing your boyfriend. But Jill had worked and saved all last summer so she could redo her bedroom. I had helped her pick out everything.

"Jill, that's terrible!"

"Lisa, would you come over? I can't face this by myself."

"Well, I don't know." I could see myself in the hall mirror. I looked as bad as I felt. I finally said I'd try to come.

I went back to my room and fell into bed. I tried to go to sleep, but couldn't.

Poor Jill. But she was lucky, too. She didn't have a boyfriend to break up with. I wanted to stay in my warm bed, but Jill had been my friend for years, and now she needed me, but if I went.....I shuddered. I'd have to tell Jill about Mike. But I had to go. Jill was depending on me.

When I rang Jill's doorbell, she rushed out. "Lisa! I was afraid you wouldn't come."

"I almost didn't," I confessed. "But you sounded so desperate."

"I am. Wait till you see what happened." We walked up the hall, and Jill threw open the door to her room. "Look."

I did. It was terrible. The striped wallpaper was bulging with big brown rain spots. "Oh, Jill!" Along one wall, her new white carpet was stained an ugly brown. "Oh, Jill," I repeated. "Oh that's really awful." It was, too. Everything was sad. I wanted to race home to my own room, but I couldn't go off and leave Jill. She sank onto her bed and sighed. "All the babysitting I did, and all the time we spent shopping."

I sat down beside her and examined the damage. I knew how much it meant to have a nice room to bring the other girls to. But maybe...my mind began working....if we moved the dresser and the desk....

"Jill, give me some paper." I began to sketch a new floor plan.

"I think we could rearrange it this way and hide the spots."

"Oh, Lisa, that looks great. I knew you'd come up with something!" Jill looked so excited, and tears came to her eyes. "Let's do it right now!"

There was no way I could leave and go home and brood about Mike. My mind returned to the room. Even if we moved the furniture, one large stain would still show. Then an idea jumped into my head. "Jill, maybe we could make a wall covering."

So we found an old white bedspread. We sat down and stitched designs on it with bright yarn. The doorbell rang while we were working. In a moment, Jill's mother came in to say that two boys from school, Jeff and Bart, were there. I wondered if they knew about Mike and me. Anyway, I was going to have to admit it. I felt almost sick.

"Hi," Jill called out. "You're just in time." We had begun to move the dresser away from the wall.

"What happened here?" Bart said from the doorway. "You must have had some leaks. That's a bummer."

Jill sighed. "I know. Isn't it awful? But Lisa knows what to do. Show them, Lisa."

Somehow I managed to speak. "Well, I made this plan." I held out the sketch and hesitated. "I think it'll look all right."

Jeff and Bart came over and studied my sketch. "Hey," Jeff said. "you have good ideas, Lisa." He had friendly blue eyes, and he smiled down at me. "Want us to help you move the furniture?"

"Yeah," said Bart. "Let us help."

"Maybe we could move the dresser over here." That was my voice speaking. "Then the bookcase there, and the desk there. Then we'll hang the wall covering over the big spot. Don't think about *him,* I told myself. Just keep going.Jill and I hurried around, moving books and lamps so we could all move the furniture. When we were finished, we stood back to view the room.

"Looks good," Jeff said.

"Oh, Lisa, thank you." Jill was happy now, smiling like her old self again.

"It's great, Lisa," Bart added. "You should work with us on the stage sets for the spring play."

Jeff looked at me for a moment. "Lisa's got no time, right, Lisa? You're always busy with Mike."

There it was. The bomb had gone off at last. But I was still in one piece. I knew now what I had to do. "Well, actually, I've got lots of time," I said. I realized that helping Jill had helped me, too. I had to keep going, get involved with others.

"You know," I said, facing all of them. "About Mike and me I told them. It wasn't as hard as I thought it would be.

THE END

GIRL RUNNER

By Martha Tolles

Three girls were hanging around Jack when I was introduced to him at the Rec Center, but I hardly noticed them. Jack's blue eyes were all I could think about.

"Hi," I smiled up at him. I had add him on the basketball and baseball teams, but up close he was even looking.

"Hi, Anne, nice to meet you," he answered. "I was just going to show Christy and Patty and Sally how to pool."

Christy picked up a cue stick. "Jack, do you hold this stick, anyway?" She snuggled up to Jack, holding the cue as if it were a broom.

While Jack bent over Christy placing fingers on the cue, I turned to Patty said, "Do you want me to show how? I've always played a lot with older brothers." But Patty gave me a really cold look and moved over to Jack. I guess he hadn't heard me because he glanced up in a minute and "You're next, Anne."

"Don't forget about me, "Sally exclaimed.

I couldn't blame her. I, too, liked the idea of having Jack help me, but I would feel silly pretending that I didn't know how.

I would have to confess.

Just then the bell rang, and the lunch period was over. So that solved one problem, but Jack turned to me and said, "Do you want a ride back to school, Anne? How did you get over here?"

I almost blurted out, "I ran," but something held me back. I didn't want tell him that I had run over to the Rec Center and planned to run back, too. Somehow I didn't want him to know that I was on the track team. I wasn't sure how Jack would take it, but I could guess what the other girls would think.

So I said, "Thanks, Jack, I'd love a ride."

On the way back to school, the three girls kept asking him questions: "Oh, Jack, who's going to win the game?" and "Jack, explain that two-base hit to me again." Jack seemed amused by their questions and laughed a lot, so I felt sure that was the type of girl he liked. I kept quiet even though I knew the answers.

When Jack let us out in the parking lot, he offered to drive us all home before he went to baseball practice. And he looked right at me when he said it. How could I miss such a chance? What expression would come over his face when I said, "Sorry, Jack, the coach is expecting me for track practice:" I knew he would be surprised, at least. People are always saying that I don't look like the athletic type.

"Thanks, Jack, I'd love it." I smiled at him, quickly figuring that I could run back to school after he dropped me off at home. I just couldn't miss this practice, because we were having our first track meet with another school tomorrow.

Co-ed sports had come to southern California this year, and it was the first time girls could take part in sports with the boys. I wasn't exactly a star on the team. In fact, I was usually one of the slowest. But I worked hard, kept in shape, and didn't miss practice. And I was improving. The coach had told us right from the beginning: "You have to shape up. No goofing off, or you'll be cut from the team." That would mean going back to gym class for calisthenics and boring things like that. Besides, I really enjoyed running. The coach kept saying he was glad to have girls "on board". He'd been in the Navy once and never quite got over it.

I met my friend Susie in the hall that afternoon and told her about Jack. "Oh, that's super, Anne!" she exclaimed. "He's just your type." But was I his? That was the big question.

During the rest of the day, I rehearsed how I'd casually mention the track team. It was silly to hide it, especially since Jack was sure to hear about it sooner or later. I could say that I had to go home for my track shoes or my running shorts. "Oh, Anne Lattimer, stop being so crazy," I scolded myself. Mom would say, "Be yourself, Anne." But how would Jack react? That's the part I wanted to put off, just for a little while, just so he could think of me as a girl, not an athlete.

After school, we all piled into Jack's jeep. "I have to hurry," he called over his shoulder, "I left my mitt at home." The jeep engine burst into a roar, and we wheeled out of the parking lot. As we drove along, the wind blew through our hair and made it look like silky fringe.

And then we were at my house.

"Thanks a lot, Jack."

"See you tomorrow, Anne. I'll meet you in the parking lot."

I waved and waited until he was gone. Then I started to run back to school. It was hot for early spring, and there wasn't much shade from the tall palms overhead. As I ran, I thought about Jack. He had said, "See you tomorrow." But when? Tomorrow? Did he mean after school? I knew he didn't have baseball practice tomorrow, but I had a track meet.

When I arrived back at school, I barely had time to get a drink of water and star breathing slowly again before the coach came out on the field. "All right, everybody. You've been sitting around all day. Let's run down to the park."

So we did, and then ran along the path that circles the park. It was a

hard work out, and afterwards we all sprawled on the grass, exhausted.

"Are you ready for the meet tomorrow, Nancy?" I asked the other girl on the team.

"Oh, I guess so," Nancy answered.

"It'll be fun, but I guess there's no way we can beat these boys."

"I know. Maybe there'll be some girls on the other team. "Then I turned to my real worry. "I wonder if anybody comes to watch these meets?"

'"Oh, some." Nancy bent to tie her shoelace. ''The word's getting around that we might have a pretty good team this year even with us on it." She laughed.

That evening the phone rang. When I lifted the receiver and heard a voice, "Hi, Anne, this is Jack," I stared in the hall mirror and smiled a huge smile. I could see tiny sparks light up my eyes.

"Jack!" I forgot to sound calm. My voice went up with excitement. "How are you?"

"O.K. Say, Anne, I wanted to tell you the team has to meet with the coach tomorrow at lunchtime, so I can't take you girls over to the Rec Center."

So now I knew he'd meant lunchtime.

"Well, we'll miss you," I said, but was actually relieved. Maybe I could still keep him from finding out about the meet.

We began to talk about the baseball game day after tomorrow. Then, all of a sudden, he said, "Could I meet you after school tomorrow? You and me? We'll go get a hamburger." I stared into the mirror in confusion

"Don't be dumb, tell him," I told myself. But if I did, he would know that I wasn't like the other girls. "Anne?" he repeated.

"Well," I laughed in a silly way, giving up. "You won't believe this, but I'm on the track team. We have a meet tomorrow. "There, it was out.There was a silence. "You what?"

Jack's voice sounded amazed. "You mean you're one of the girls out for track?" How I wished I could see his face. "Are you kidding me?"

"No, I'm not kidding." I used my brightest voice. "It's-it's really lots of fun."

"Well, listen, okay then. My mom wants the phone so I have to get off. Good-bye, Anne."

"Good-bye, Jack-and thanks." The phone went click, and I hung up slowly. When I decided to go out for track, I had no idea it would mean turning down a date with Jack McCarty.

All evening I couldn't shake my sadness. When I woke the next morning, that heavy feeling was still there, like a blanket.

I dragged off to school. I told Susie about it before Biology, but she didn't seem to understand at all. She just kept saying, "He asked you to go out for a hamburger that's really super, Anne." I saw Jack in the distance, in the hall later. He waved. What a smile he had! But I would never forget the surprise I'd heard in his voice last evening.

After school, I went to the locker room and got into my track clothes. Nancy was there, already dressed. "Hurry," she called. "Anne, I heard Bella Vista isn't all that great."

"Oh, really?" I pulled on my shorts.

I didn't care at all, but I tried not to let on.

I walked to the track with Nancy as she talked about the other team. I sat on the bench while the coach gave us a pep talk. I could be in Jack's car now, my hair floating in the air like soft fringe. I could e looking up into his eyes-if only I Hadn't decided to go out for this team, to be different from the kind of girl that jack liked. I gazed at the blue mountains off to the north wile I thought about it. My brothers had urged me to do it. They were good guys, but what did they know? Half of the time, they treat me like another boy.

"All right, now," the coach was saying. "Let's get in there and give it all you've got." "I already have," I thought, and glanced toward the parking lot where the cars were moving out of their slots and down the driveway to the street. And there was the bitterest sight of all, Jack's jeep. He was at the wheel, with Christy next to him, and Patty and Sally in the back. I stared with jealous eyes as they joined the line of traffic and drove off down the street.

I watched the relays and the two mile and in a glazed sort of way. I felt only half there; the other half had gone off in the jeep with Jack and the girls. Then, we were lining up for the six-sixty, Nancy, three boys and I. I saw slender, tanned legs and a pair of smallish track shoes below my own-and I hated them. The sharp crack of the starting gun split the air. I dug in. You as well try to be at something, a voice was saying the depths of my mind. And I took off down the track for my first lap. I looked at the Bella Vista runner just ahead of me. is feet were hitting the dirt track hard. I could hear him breathing. His arms were cramped in a tight position up close to his chest, and his stride seemed slower. He looked out of shape. I'd gone to every practice, starting weeks before the season.

I sucked in even gulps of air as we completed the first time around the track and started on the last lap. There were voices and shouts in my ears from the few spectators. My feet felt light. Pretend you're a doctor, I told myself. You're on your way to a dying patient. Hurry! Hurry! I passed something on my right. I flung my whole body across the gauze tape at the finish line, y chest heaving. I'd beaten the guy from Bella Vista!

The coach and the other players were around me, patting me on the back. I'd come in this, and we needed every point. Oh, but I was tired. I sank onto the nearest bench to rest a minute while the teams got ready for the eight-eighty. I glanced up and saw Jack McCarty walking toward me. I blinked my eyes. I must be hallucinating from sheer exhaustion. But the miracle came closer and smiled and even sat down beside me. Jack's arm was around me, hugging me, his blue eyes looking into mine. Surely he couldn't be hugging a winded, perspiring girl runner? But he was.

"Jack," I burst out.

"Anne." Was that admiration in those blue eyes? "You were far out, girl Did you ever look good!"

Look good! This guy was incredible. But if that's what he wanted to think.

"I'm really tired." I sagged against him, resting my head on his shoulder.

"Where're Christy and the other?"

"I dropped them off on my way home." He moved a little closer. "you know, I thought you were like the other girls."

THE END

SWIM MEET
By Martha Tolles

Emmy raced across the park toward the swimming pool. "I'll beat you in, Jacob," she shouted at her brother. Even though he was two years older, she wanted to prove she could keep up. But by the time she'd slipped into the water, Jacob was already diving down deep, then coming up for air.

"Bet you can't do that," he shouted.

"I don't want to." She quickly flipped over onto her back and backstroked away from him. She'd show him what a great swimmer she was.

"Aw, Emmy. Put your face in the water," he called after her. "The way we did in swim class. You know how."

Emmy liked her way better. Besides, when she put her face in the water, there was so much to worry about. Would she swallow it? Would she forget to breathe through her nose? Would the water get in her eyes even though she wore goggles?

She started to paddle over to some twin girls. The twins called to her, "Do you want to play with us? Watch." They tossed blue and yellow rings down to the bottom of the pool, then diving down to get them. Emmy was horrified. She could never go way underwater like that.

"Can't right now," she called back. "I have to practice," and she backstroked off down the pool, her face nice and dry. But she felt lonely.

Just then she noticed that Jacob and some others had climbed out of the pool and were over by a bulletin board. Their swim teacher, Connie, was tacking up a big poster. Emmy splashed across the pool to join them.

"Swim Meet," the poster read. "Ribbons for winners."

"I want to sign up too," Emmy told Jacob. "I want to win a ribbon, just like you."

All that week, Emmy practiced for the swim meet. Jacob did too. One day, their neighbor, Mrs. Hernand, invited Emmy and Jacob and their mom to swim in her pool. Jacob dove into the water and surfaced. "Come on, Emmy, try to put your face in," he urged her.

Just then, Mrs. Hernand's pup jumped into the pool and paddled across.

"See how he swims?" Emmy shouted triumphantly. "He keeps his nose and eyes out of the water just like me. He's a smart dog."

"Emmy-y-y, you're not a dog. Mom, tell her to swim some other strokes."

"Give her time, Jacob. See how well she does the backstroke."

Finally, it was Saturday, the day of the swim meet. They loaded up the car and drove to Lamanda Park. Emmy was amazed to see long lines of cars and crowds of people. Jacob joked, "They've all come to watch us swim. Are you ready, Emmy?"

Emmy felt tightness in her stomach. She wasn't really sure.

As they made their way through crowds, Emmy saw how different the pool looked, all divided up into lanes by long ropes. They had just settled down on a blanket when a voice on the loud speaker blared out some words.

"Did you hear that?" Jacob jumped up. "It's time for me to swim. They called all the 7-year-olds." He grabbed his swim goggles and dashed off.

"Good luck, good luck," Mom and Emmy called. They jumped up too and hurried over to the edge of the pool where they could watch the race.

The boys lined up at the deep end. In a minute, the starting horn blew.

The boys dove in and came streaking down the pool, their arms flashing in the sun. Jacob seemed to be in the lead.

Everyone was screaming, "Go, Lamanda! Go fast! Beat Stratford!"

"Faster, Jacob," Emma screeched, leaping up and down. She was thrilled for her team, proud of her brother.

At the shallow end, the swimmers climbed out, dripping and breathing hard. It was difficult to tell who was first. "Maybe you won, Jacob," Emmy shouted, rushing over and hugging him.

"That'll help your team, whether you were first, second or third," Mom added, smiling and wrapping him in a towel. "You'll get a ribbon for sure."

In a moment, a loud voice called out the results. Jacob had come in first. Emmy wanted to do well too.

Finally, it was time for the 5-year-old girls. Mom and Jacob walked to the deep end of the pool with Emmy. Emmy peered down into the depths of the water. Would she have to get her face in the water? "You're a good swimmer, a strong swimmer, Emmy. Don't worry," Mom assured her. "Yeah, go for it," Jacob said. "Help us win the meet." But Emmy wasn't sure she could. Still, she longed to help, longed to win a ribbon too.

The 5-year-old swimmers were gathered in a big bunch. The twins Emmy had seen the other days were there too. The swim teacher Connie beckoned to Emmy.

"Over here. There are two groups. You'll be in the second one, Emmy. Ready for the backstroke, everyone?" Emmy didn't feel very ready.

Connie, the swim teacher, called out: "Now it's time for you girls. Do your best." Emmy shivered with excitement and worry and moved to the edge of the pool. The twins and the others jumped in, splashing happily, going underwater and getting their faces wet. Emmy pulled her goggles on and slid into the water, keeping her face nice and dry. Then, like the others, she gripped the edge of the pool in a crouching position, her feet planted against the side, and waited for the horn.

The horn blasted through the air. Emmy shoved off on her back, her arms flailing rapidly as she stared at the blue sky overhead. Fast, faster, she must go. Her feet kicked hard. The water rippled over her body. She was doing great, wasn't she?

But what was the matter? She had bumped into something. She had hit the rope. Her arm and leg were caught in it. Water sloshed into her face from the other swimmers. "Help, oh, help." She clung to the rope, fighting to remember how to breathe. She mustn't choke. Finally, she managed to untangle herself, turning round and round. At last, she was clear of the rope. She must hurry. But Emmy hadn't reached the far end of the pool. Voices were yelling. "Stop, stop. Turn around. You went the wrong way."

Through her swim goggles, Emmy stared up in horror at her swim teacher and the other girls at the edge of the pool. She was back at the starting point. "Go the other way," people shouted at her.

What a mess. What should she do? "Swim, Emmy, swim," Connie called out to her. Emmy felt like climbing out of the pool. But instead, she took a deep breath, flipped herself around and started off backstroking again.

Were the others way ahead of her?

By the time Emmy backstroked to the far end of the pool, she was really tired. And she saw that she was the very last one in any of the swim lanes. No one else was in the pool. How terrible. But all the people lined up around the pool were cheering and clapping and smiling at her. Why? And there was Jacob with Mom right behind him.

"Way to go, Em," Jacob shouted. "You kept at it."

Mom leaned over the edge of the pool toward her.

"Good work, Emmy dear. That was a lot of good swimming. You'll win a ribbon for that."

THE END

THE BEST THING ALL WEEK

By Martha Tolles

Ginny hurried beneath the tall pines toward Karen and Anne's cabin. They had to be there. Of course they would wait for her, wouldn't they?

"Hi!" Ginny knocked on their door, already smiling at the thought of seeing them again. But there was no answer.

"They went to play tennis, "the girl in the next cabin said.

Ginny hurried back to her cabin. Maybe they would be there waiting for her. But when she reached her cabin, only her roommate, Marybelle, was there unpacking her clothes.

"Did my friends come?" Ginny asked breathlessly, but Marybelle shook her head. Ginny grabbed her racket and rushed out the door. But when she got down to the courts, she found that Karen and Anne were already playing with two other girls.

"We couldn't find you," they called, waving happily. Ginny walked slowly back to her cabin. Marybelle was there writing postcards. Ginny finished putting away her clothes. She thought about how she would try to sit with Anne and Karen at supper. But when she got to the dining hall, Karen and Anne were already seated at the long table while she was still far back in line.

Finally, around the campfire that evening, she caught up with them. It was great to be back with her friends again.

"It's a shame we couldn't be in the same cabin, "Anne said, moving over to let Ginny sit in the middle.

"It is, Karen agreed. "What's your roommate like?"

"Oh, I don't know. "Ginny shrugged. "She doesn't say much or do much. "Ginny hadn't really thought about her. "I'd rather be with you guys. "She smiled at her friends.

The next day was just the same. Most of the time it was difficult for the three of them to get together.

During their swimming time in the lake, the girls had to be partners with their roommates. When Anne and Karen saw her with Marybelle, they made sad faces as if they missed her. But then they seemed to have a lot of fun laughing and splashing around in the water together.

"Do you want to go swimming?" Marybelle asked Ginny.

"Oh, OK, "Ginny said. She and Marybelle swam around some, but Ginny kept trying to stay close to Anne and Karen.

Ginny began to wish she hadn't come to camp. This was the trip she and her friends had planned all winter. And now look at it. What fun was a camp without friends? That afternoon she wrote to her mother and said the food wasn't very good and neither was camp. Her mother was sure to be sorry for her, wasn't she? She walked over to the office to mail her letter. As she was returning down the row of cabins, she saw Marybelle sitting on their doorstep. How sad she looked! Then she rubbed her arm over her eyes as if she might be crying. Ginny felt suddenly almost cross. Marybelle should be enjoying camp and making friends and having fun and....

Ginny stood still and stared down at the dirt path for a minute. Those words flew around in her brain making friends, having fun. Then she began to run. "Marybelle," she shouted. "Come on! Let's go do something. Do you want to?"

Marybelle raised her head with a surprised look, but then she smiled. "Sure," she said. And Marybelle's smile was the best thing Ginny had seen all week.

THE END

SPECIAL VALENTINE

Written for News Trails by Martha Tolles

Wendy carried her valentines to school carefully. She had cards for all her friends and a very special big one for Mary Lou, the most popular girl in the class.

As Wendy hurried along, she peeped in the paper sack again for another glimpse at the special valentine. She had made it out of red paper and bits of real white lace, shiny cellophane, and tiny candy hearts. Mary Lou was sure to love it and ask Wendy to play during recess.

During the morning the class worked very hard so that they would be ready for their valentine party. They hardly looked up when Christina's mother came in with a big box of cup cakes for the class.

Christina was the new girl in their room. Wendy suddenly remembered that she hadn't brought Christina any valentine at all. Christina was so very quiet, and her English was often difficult to understand because she was from another country. Christina didn't know how to play their games, and she hardly ever talked at all, so somehow, she was always being left out. Wendy eyed Christina's blonde braids and for a moment was sorry she had not brought her a valentine. But the thought of her special big one for Mary Lou made her heart dance.

After lunch Miss Pringle served the cup cakes and explained to the class that Christina had helped her mother make them. They were fluffy, delicious yellow cakes.

Then Miss Pringle collected all the valentines and stood up front to pass them out. One after another she handed them out. 14 Mary Lou's pile grew faster than anybody's. Christina's pile grew very slowly. In fact, from what Wendy could see, it didn't look like a pile at all, just a few cards. Christina's face looked sad, and Wendy wished she had brought her one.

Finally, Miss Pringle picked up the big, red heart edged with lace, and she stood, examining the card, turning it over and over.

"But there's no name on this card." She exclaimed. "Who is it for? Who sent it?" and she held it high so the whole class could see it. Every one let out a long "oh-h-h-h."

"Oh, my," Wendy gasped, realizing she must have forgotten to write her name on it. She raised her hand. All the faces turned eagerly toward her. A hush fell over the class, and it seemed as though every pair of eyes was saying, "Is it for me?" Except for Christina, who sat with folded hands.

"It's my card," Wendy said. Then unexpected words tumbled from her lips, words that she hadn't known she was going to say.

"The card is for Christina," she added proudly. A murmur went up from the class, and she could see the surprise on Christina's face.

"How nice," said Miss Pringle as she handed the card to Christina.

Right away an admiring circle of children gathered around Christina's desk. By the time Wendy reached her, she was busily handing out one tiny candy hearts to everyone.

"Thank you," she called out to Wendy. More children crowd around to get a good look at the valentine.

"Hold it up, Christina," they called out. "Let us see it, too."

A moment later the recess bell rang, but the children continued to stand over Christina's desk. As Wendy turned to the door she saw Mary Lou, still sitting at her desk.

"Wait, Wendy," she called, getting up. "What a beautiful valentine you gave Christina! Tell me how you made it." And she slipped her arm through Wendy's as they walked off together.

THE END

BEN'S BIG YEAR

Martha Tolles is the author of eight middle grade novels published by Scholastic, (over two million copies sold) including Who's Reading Darci's Diary and Katie and Those Boys. Two of them, Darci in Cabin 13 and Marrying Off Mom, were selected for the IRA Children's Choices reading list. She is also the author of two dozen short stories and three chapter books. She and her lawyer husband had five boys and one girl. She is a graduate of Smith College.

Ben's Big Year..."a regular kid who has an endearing zest for life"... "Family love shines through in these timeless anecdotes..." Kirkus Reviews

Growing Up Stories are about boys and girls who learn how to handle many experiences, from scaring away a bear, to keeping a dog safe while on a camping trip, to dealing with different kinds of friends.

41489289R00044

Made in the USA
Charleston, SC
29 April 2015